MW00901442

Copyright Material

The Adventures of Jabbo & Dabbo: A Rainbow Adventure
Text copyright ©2020 by Jessica Triplett-Ward. All rights reserved. No part of this book may be reproduced or transmitted in any form or by any means, electronic, or mechanical, including recording, or by any information storage and retrieval system, without written permission from the author, except by a reviewer who may quote brief passages in a review.

For more information visit: Jessy Triplett-Ward onf Facebook @authorjessytriplettward

Illustrations by: Polina Hrytskova

Interior and Cover Build by Infinity Flower Publishing, LLC
www.infinityflowerpublishing.com

ISBN 978-1-0879341-4-3 (hardback)

4

THE ADVENTURES
OF
JABBO AND DABBO:
A Rainbow Adventure

Written By: Jessy Triplett-Ward & Renee Weede

Illustrated By: Polina Hrytskova

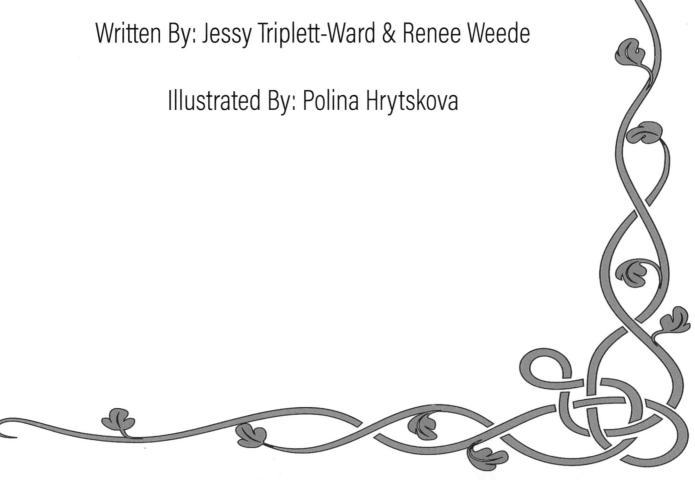

This book is dedicated in memory to Augusta Mayo Fullen and Laverne Fullen-Kiff.
To Judah, Elijah, and Samuel, thank you for being my first audience, my biggest fans, and for
helping make this book what it is. I love you three so very much.
To my Mom, this would not be possible without you. I love you.

Genesis 9:16

Foreword

The story of Jabbo and Dabbo has been passed down in my family throughout generations. It all started with my Great-Grandma, Augusta Mayo Fullen. She is the original heart of this story. She would tell these stories to my Grandma, Laverne Fullen-Kiff, and the tradition passed down. It is amazing to see this story become a book – something to hold on to and share. The stories of Jabbo and Dabbo mean so much to my family and I hope they become a special part of yours.

Augusta Mayo Fullen

Laverne Fullen-Kiff

In the land of milk and honey, a small cabin sat tucked away, right next to a large forest that backed right up to huge mountains covered in snow. When the sun would rise or set, it would make the road to the cabin look like golden honey. The cabin was the home of Momma Bear and her two cubs, Jabbo and Dabbo.

One day, Momma Bear went to wake up Jabbo and Dabbo for breakfast. "Wake up my little ones," Momma Bear said.

Jabbo did not mind early mornings and would always wake up with wide eyes ready for adventure. Dabbo, on the other hand, grabbed his pillow and put it over his head.

"Do we have to?" Dabbo complained. "Momma, just five more minutes."

"I made honey porridge for breakfast," Momma Bear softly whispered in Dabbo's ears. Both cubs ran quickly to the kitchen.

Momma Bear made the best honey porridge. The two cubs sat at the table, waiting patiently for the honey topping. Momma Bear went to pour the honey out, but there was none. Not even a drop left!

"Oh, no! I'm out of honey," Momma Bear said.

"That's ok Momma, we will eat this and go on an adventure to find some more!" Jabbo excitedly exclaimed.

Momma Bear chuckled. "Ok, but you have to be back by sunset," said Momma Bear. "I'll be making my honey cakes for dessert!"

The two cubs ran out of the cabin and quickly made it down the golden road into the lush green forest. Birds chirped, proud and loud. The squirrels rushed up and down the tree trunks, looking for food. Everything seemed so alive. The forest had its own music. Dabbo heard the sound of buzzing of bees in the air.

"I think I found the spot," cried out Dabbo to Jabbo.

"I'll climb to get the honey this time," Jabbo said.

He was only able to get one jar of honey before he felt the first drop of rain. Down the tree Jabbo went and the two brothers ran off to find shelter from the rain.

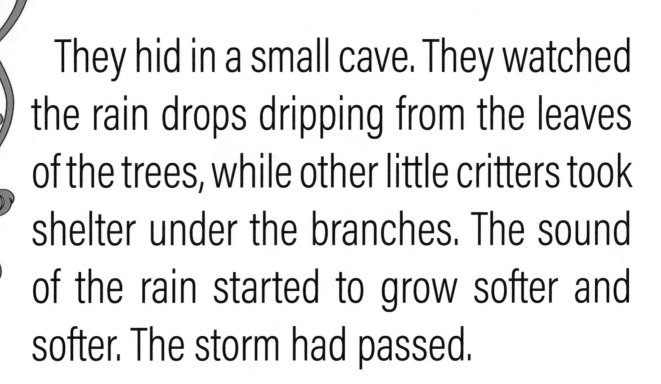

They hid in a small cave. They watched the rain drops dripping from the leaves of the trees, while other little critters took shelter under the branches. The sound of the rain started to grow softer and softer. The storm had passed.

The two bears started their journey back home, but they saw a huge rainbow. The rainbow had so many pretty colors and it reached as high as their eyes could see.

"I wonder if we can climb this rainbow?" Jabbo asked Dabbo.

"We can try," said Dabbo.

"Race you!" shouted Jabbo as he took off toward the rainbow, holding the jar of honey.

They started running, then running upwards! They were on the rainbow.

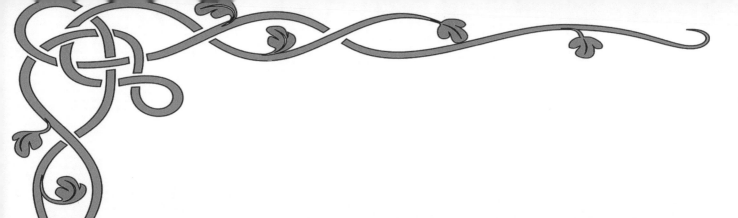

As they reached the top, Dabbo paused since he was out of breath.

"This is amazing," Dabbo said in awe.

"Ready to slide down?" Jabbo asked.

The two cubs slid down the rainbow and into a giant pot of honey! There was enough honey at the end of the rainbow for the coming winter months.

The cubs were covered in honey goo and ate their fill. Jabbo and Dabbo were able to get all the jars filled to take home to Momma. They couldn't wait to tell Momma their story!

Momma Bear was amazed at how much honey Jabbo and Dabbo brought home. She gave them a huge hug.

"I'll make the honey cakes now and you two tell me all about your adventure," Momma Bear said.

Jabbo and Dabbo told Momma Bear all of what happened. After they all ate honey cakes, it was time for bed.

As Momma Bear tucked them into bed, Jabbo and Dabbo both said, "We can't wait to go on another adventure tomorrow!"

"Goodnight, Momma," they said.

"Goodnight," said Momma Bear.

The End

About the Authors:

Jessy Triplett-Ward lives in La Marque, TX with her three boys and four forever rescues. She holds a Bachelors Degree in Nursing and works full time as a registered nurse. When not working, she is actively pursuing her Masters Degree in Nurse Leadership, painting, singing, and writing. She looks forward to writing more and providing memories for many households.

Renee Weede resides in Hitchcock with her husband, Allen. She is a retired operator and laboratory analyst. She has a passion for art and writing. She's Jessy's mother and best friend.

CPSIA information can be obtained
at www.ICGtesting.com
Printed in the USA
BVHW011013020323
659555BV00009B/552